Julie—

Thank you so much for your
support!

Wishing you a lifetime of
love! ♡ ♡♡

mia and jake

This book is dedicated to my friends and family who strapped in and rode the sometimes bumpy but never boring "love rollercoaster" with me all the way to finding Lucas, my One.

For more information about Mia and Jake please visit
www.miaandjake.com

Sea Hill Press, Inc.
P. O. Box 60301
Santa Barbara, CA 93160

www.seahillpress.com
ISBN: 978-1-937720-09-4
Printed in Hong Kong

mia and jake

jake

finding the one

Sherri Starr

Illustrated By Robbie Hildebrand

This is Mia.

Mia is a pretty happy girl.

She has great friends, a supportive family, a satisfying job, and is quite passionate about life in general.

But there's one thing that has continued to elude Mia ...

finding "The One."

Mia called her happily married girls for advice,

which left her even more confused.

"YOU'RE TOO PICKY."

"YOU'RE TRYING TOO HARD."

"YOU'RE NOT PICKY ENOUGH."

"YOU'RE NOT TRYING HARD ENOUGH."

Then Mia remembered some useful advice.

So Mia went to a meditation retreat

and a yoga retreat,

and she read lots of
self-help/relationship-y books

to make herself whole and complete so she'll be ready when "The One" crosses her path.

But he didn't.

Mia wondered ...

So she went to the gym

and went on a diet

and got a makeover.

But still, he was nowhere in sight.

Then Mia got an idea!

She packed up and moved to a bigger city to better her chances of finding "The One."

Mia loved her new city.

Then Mia had an idea!

But Mia didn't seem to find anyone who sparked her interest.

and blind dates.

She hired a life coach to help her with a strategy for finding "The One."

"IF YOU USE THESE TOOLS, YOU WILL HAVE SUCCESS!"

He taught her about positive thinking

and affirmations

and law of attraction.

"IF I CAN VIVIDLY IMAGINE IT, I CAN CREATE IT."

But still, "The One" was not in her life.

So Mia called her guy friends

and thought their advice
was worth a shot.

"SMILE."

"BE AGGRESSIVE."

"GIVE THEM
SIGNS."

"SOME MEN LIKE
BITCHES."

So she tried smiling at them

and being more aggressive,

and she gave them signs
that she liked them.

She even tried being bitchy.

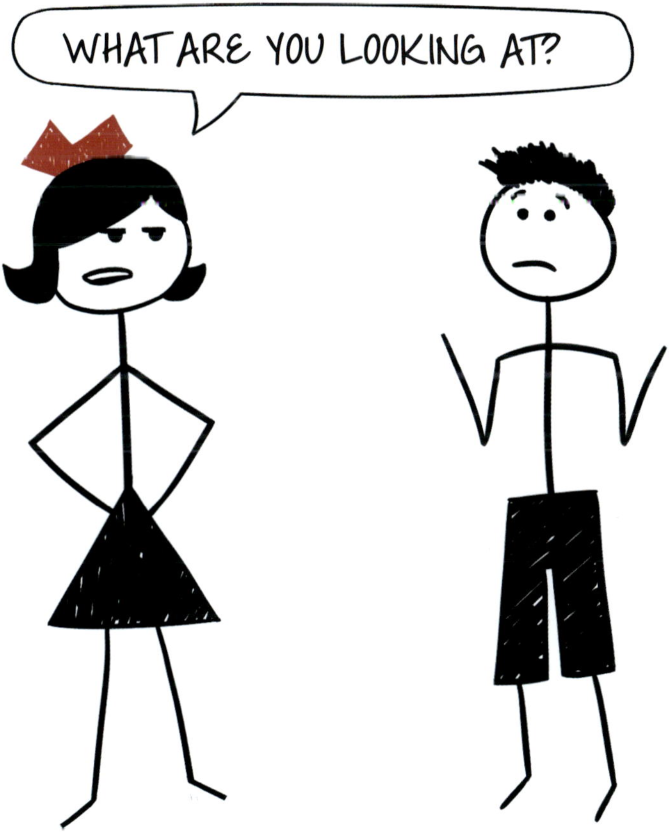

Then Mia had an idea!

She wrote a list of qualities she's looking for in a man so she can recognize "The One" when she sees him.

So Mia became more selective.

Until one day, after having tried everything she could think of to find "The One," Mia finally gave up.

and decided to focus on having
a fulfilling life on her own.

she took up tennis

and went back to school

and expressed her musical side

and spent lots of time with
her friends and family.

Mia really was happy!

She even went on a vacation
with her girlfriends.

While in Mexico, a funny thing happened.

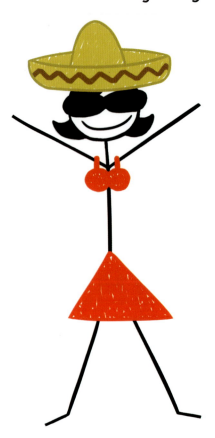

Since Mia wasn't analyzing her life anymore,

and since she wasn't asking that
nagging question, "where is he?!"...

the love she had worked
so hard to find, found her.

To be continued ...

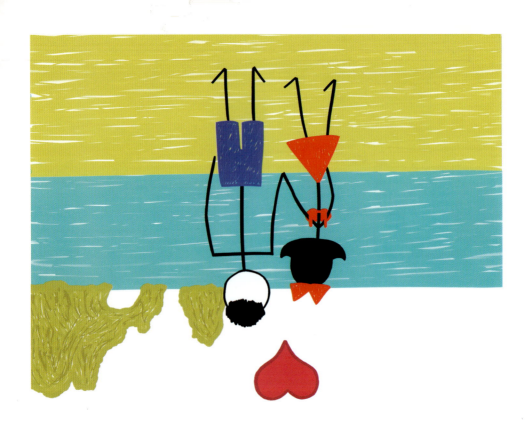

It turned out that "The one" was not only a possibility,
but a reality and well worth the wait.

And when Jake stopped daydreaming and finally got the courage to get to know her ...

Jake wondered if "love at first sight" was really possible. He was certain this was his girl.

She seemed to be cute, smart, funny, sweet and a bit nerdy. Yep, she had it all.

While in Mexico, Jake spotted a girl.

This wasn't just any girl. She was different.

and even traveled out of
the country for work.

and hanging out with his buddies

and fishing

But Jake held firm to the image of what he knew he would find one day and forgot about it.

But the girls he met didn't quite match what he was looking for.

So he decided to give online dating a shot.

Jake wondered if maybe his belief that he didn't have to work to find "The One" was flawed.

and watching them get married again.

and hanging out with his buddies ...

and fishing

So Jake spent his time surfing

and just hadn't come across her yet.

But the truth is, Jake had a clear image of exactly what he wanted ...

People began to speculate.

But sadly, those days were fleeting. Before long, Jake found himself alone again.

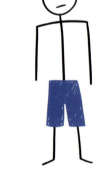

They even took turns being
each others' wingmen.

Jake liked spending more time with them.

Now that his buddies were
free again, life was great!

and hanging out with his buddies ...

and fishing

So Jake spent his time surfing

so he forgot about it.

and concluded marriage doesn't look very fun after all.

and confusing

and thought they looked exhausting

so he observed his buddies' relationships

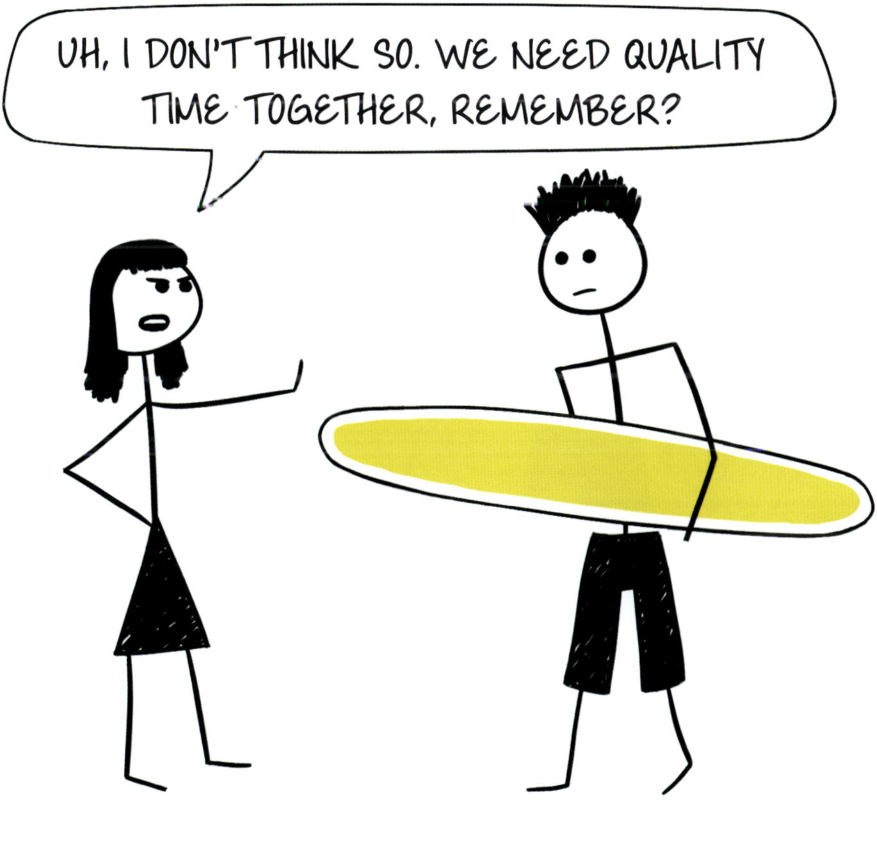

But Jake wondered if marriage was really all it was cracked up to be.

and his buddies' wives.

and hanging out with his buddies ...

and fishing

Then Jake remembered what he always believed to be true.

which was well-intended
but not very helpful.

"DUDE, YOUR
STANDARDS ARE
TOO HIGH."

"YOU'RE NO GEORGE
CLOONEY, YA KNOW?"

Jake's married buddies were
quick to offer advice,

finding "The One."

But there's one thing that has eluded Jake ...

Jake is a great catch.

This is Jake.

mia and jake

finding the one

Sherri Starr

Illustrated By Robbie Hildebrand

This book is dedicated to my friends and family who strapped in and rode the sometimes bumpy but never boring "love rollercoaster" with me all the way to finding Lucas, my One.

For more information about Mia and Jake please visit www.miaandjake.com

Sea Hill Press, Inc.
P. O. Box 60301
Santa Barbara, CA 93160

www.seahillpress.com
ISBN: 978-1-937720-09-4
Printed in Hong Kong

mia and jake